Miley
the Stylist
Fairy

Special thanks to
Narinder Dhami

ORCHARD BOOKS
338 Euston Road, London NW1 3BH
Orchard Books Australia
Level 17/207 Kent Street, Sydney, NSW 2000
A Paperback Original

First published in 2012 by Orchard Books

HiT entertainment

A CIP catalogue record for this book is available
from the British Library.

ISBN 978 1 40831 592 7

3 5 7 9 10 8 6 4

Printed in Great Britain

The paper and board used in this paperback are natural recyclable
products made from wood grown in sustainable forests. The
manufacturing processes conform to the environmental regulations
of the country of origin.

Orchard Books is a division of Hachette Children's Books,
an Hachette UK company

www.hachette.co.uk

Miley
the Stylist
Fairy

by Daisy Meadows

ORCHARD

www.rainbowmagic.co.uk

Jack Frost's Spell

It's high time for the world to see
The legend I was born to be.
The prince of pop, a dazzling star
My fans will flock from near and far.

But pop star fame is hard to get
Unless I help myself, I bet.
I need a plan, a cunning trick
To make my stage act super-slick.

Seven magic clefs I'll steal
They'll give me pop star powers, I feel.
I'll sing and dance, I'll dazzle and shine
And pop star glory will be mine!

Contents

Clashing Clothes

"What's that noise?" Rachel murmured sleepily. She could hear a steady *pitter-patter* sound on the roof of the tent above her. Yawning, Rachel sat up in her sleeping bag. At the same moment, her best friend Kirsty stirred and opened her eyes.

"Oh, it's *raining*!" Rachel exclaimed, suddenly realising what the noise was.

Kirsty sat up, too. "Is that thunder?" she asked a little nervously as a loud rumbling echoed through the tent.

Rachel laughed. "No, that's my dad snoring in the other bedroom!" she explained. Scrambling out of her sleeping bag, she went over to the tent's main entrance. Kirsty followed, and together the two girls peered out.

The site of the Rainspell Island Music Festival was awash with heavy rain. The sky was dark and threatening, and the grassy fields where the tents, stages and pop stars' trailers had been set up were already turning to mud.

"What a shame!"
Kirsty remarked,
"Especially
when we
had such
brilliant weather
yesterday."

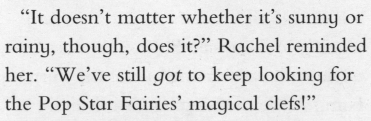

"It doesn't matter whether it's sunny or rainy, though, does it?" Rachel reminded her. "We've still *got* to keep looking for the Pop Star Fairies' magical clefs!"

Kirsty nodded. "I wonder which fairy we'll be helping today?" she said.

When the girls had arrived on Rainspell the day before, they'd discovered that Jack Frost and his goblins had stolen the Pop Star Fairies' clefs, the magical items that helped them look after pop music.

It was Jack Frost's ambition to be the richest and most famous pop star in the whole world, and he planned to use the power of the clefs to perform at the Rainspell Festival. Rachel and Kirsty had promised to help the fairies get the clefs back because without them, pop music in both the human and the fairy worlds would be spoilt for everyone. So far the girls, along with Jessie the Lyrics Fairy, Adele the Singing Coach Fairy and Vanessa the Dance Steps Fairy, had managed to rescue three of the clefs from the goblins who were hiding them.

"We saw three fantastic concerts yesterday, didn't we?" Rachel remarked as she and Kirsty went back to their sleeping area. "It was lucky Jessie, Adele and Vanessa got their clefs back in time,

and that they each had *just* enough
magic for The Angels, A-OK and Sasha
Sharp to perform."

"But the Pop Star Fairies need *all* the
clefs for things to be right again," Kirsty
sighed. "And although we've seen the
goblins, we still haven't found Jack Frost!
I wish we knew where he was hiding."

Rachel glanced at her watch. "We'd better get dressed," she said, "We're supposed to be meeting The Angels for a pancake brunch at the Harbour Cafe, remember?" The girls had become friends with famous pop group The Angels after winning a competition to meet them, and Lexy, Emilia and Serena had invited Rachel and Kirsty to the Rainspell Festival as their special guests.

Kirsty and Rachel went over to the corner of their sleeping area where they'd put their squashy bags full of clothes. Suddenly Kirsty gave a gasp as a raindrop hit her on the nose.

"Where did *that* come from?" Kirsty asked, glancing upwards. To her dismay, she saw a small tear in the tent canvas. Rain was leaking through and falling onto the bags directly underneath.

"Our bags are soaked!" Rachel groaned.

"And that means our clothes are probably soaked too," sighed Kirsty. She opened her bag and pulled out a couple of wet T-shirts. "Yes, they are!"

15

"We must have *something* dry enough to wear." Rachel began burrowing urgently through the damp contents of her own bag. "We can't meet The Angels in our pyjamas!"

The girls began to search through their clothes.

"The things at the bottom of my bag are still dry," Kirsty said. She pulled out a long pink skirt printed with yellow flowers and a green T-shirt with white spots. "I'll have to wear these, but they don't exactly go together!"

"Mine neither!" Rachel said with a grin, holding up a pair of purple and white stripy leggings and a red tartan shirt. "But they're all I've got."

Quickly the girls dressed in their mismatched outfits. They looked at each other and burst out laughing.

"Oh, well, I suppose rain and mud and funny clothes are all part of being at a music festival," Kirsty said. "And I think we ought to take a picture of ourselves!"

She grabbed her
camera and,
holding it out
in front of her,
she took a
snap of herself
and Rachel.

"At least
we have rain
macs, umbrellas
and wellies, too,"
said Rachel.

The girls put on their
plastic macs and both of them slipped
their cameras into their pockets. Then,
pulling on their wellies, they headed out.
On the way, they called to Rachel's
parents in the other sleeping area and
warned them about the leak.

"Your dad and I will sort it out while you're gone," Mrs Walker promised. "We'll see you at the concert later."

Rachel and Kirsty stepped out of the tent into the pouring rain.

"I hope it stops for the concert this afternoon," Rachel remarked, struggling to put her umbrella up in the strong breeze.

Kirsty opened her umbrella, too. Immediately a shower of rainbow-coloured glitter tumbled out, followed by a tiny fairy.

"It's Miley the Stylist Fairy!" Kirsty cried.

At the Harbour Cafe

Miley smiled at the girls, shaking the dazzling fairy dust from her long brown hair. She wore a denim mini-skirt with leggings and a blue hoodie, and sparkly orange trainers.

"Isn't this weather awful, girls?" Miley cried, hovering under the shelter of Kirsty's umbrella. "Of course you know why I'm here – to find my magical musical clef. Without it, all the pop stars' special, stylish clothes will be ruined!"

"Yes, it would be terrible if the pop stars have to wear silly outfits like the ones Kirsty and I have on!" Rachel agreed. "We're just on our way to meet The Angels at the Harbour Cafe, Miley."

"So we can look out for your clef on the way," Kirsty added.

"Wonderful!" Miley beamed at them. "I'll keep out of sight up here." And she fluttered up to the top of Kirsty's umbrella and perched on one of the spokes.

The girls began to make their way across the festival site.

Although it was raining so heavily, people were still out and about in wellies and raincoats.

"Star Village is just as busy as usual in spite of the rain," Rachel remarked as they trudged through the mud. Star Village was a group of tents where people could try out different pop star activities like dressing up, karaoke and learning dance routines.

Suddenly Kirsty caught Rachel's arm. "Keep away from those boys over there, Rachel," she murmured. "They're splashing everyone with mud!"

Rachel glanced around and saw a gang of boys wearing long, bright green macs, large rain-hats pulled down over their faces and huge

wellies. The boys were pretending to perform a dance routine, but Rachel could see that they were just jumping about in the puddles and spattering everyone who went past with muddy water.

"Thanks, Kirsty," Rachel said as they walked on, keeping well away from the mischievous boys. "Someone's going to get really annoyed with them in a minute!"

The girls carried on through the festival site, keeping a lookout for the magical musical clef. But there was no sign of it, and they didn't see any goblins either. They left the site and went on to the Harbour Cafe which was situated in Rainspell's pretty little harbour overlooking the sandy beach.

When they reached the cafe, the girls stopped under the red and white striped awning to close their umbrellas. Miley whizzed out and tucked herself neatly out of sight inside the pocket of Rachel's tartan shirt.

"Look, Rachel." Kirsty pointed with the tip of her umbrella at a colourful poster stuck in the cafe window. "It's Groove Gang! I can't wait to see their concert this afternoon."

"Don't they look brilliant?" Rachel said, studying the poster. The five members of Groove Gang always wore their own special colour – Yvette wore a yellow hoodie and trainers, Rick wore red, Blake blue, Lila lilac and Priya was pretty in pink. The same five colours had been used in swirling patterns all over the background of the poster.

"Those are the outfits they wear in the music video for *A Style of Your Own*," said Rachel. "I love that song!"

"Me, too," Kirsty agreed. "I hope they sing it this afternoon."

Rachel pushed open the cafe door and the girls went inside.

"Rachel, Kirsty!" called Lexy, one of The Angels, from a table in the big bay window. "Come and join us."

The girls hurried towards Serena, Emilia and Lexy. But The Angels weren't alone. Sitting with them were five teenagers wearing brown hoodies.

"Kirsty, it's Groove Gang!" Rachel whispered excitedly as they approached the table. "Looks like we're having brunch with *two* pop bands instead of one!"

"Fantastic!" Kirsty murmured, her eyes shining. Then she frowned. "But they look so different from the poster. I wonder why they aren't wearing their special colours today?"

Drabby Dressers

"Glad you could make it, girls," said Serena with a smile as Kirsty and Rachel sat down. "I'm sure you recognise our friends, Groove Gang?"

"Of course we do!" Kirsty said a little shyly. "Rachel and I *love* your music videos. We're always trying to copy your dance moves!"

"Our favourite is *A Style of Your Own*," Rachel added.

Lila smiled at the girls. "Thank you," she said. "We love meeting our fans."

"It's a bit embarrassing, though," Blake said, pulling a face, "Because we don't have a lot of style today at all!" And he glanced down at his brown hoodie.

"We had an accident with the washing-machine this morning," explained Priya. "Our stylist, Suzy Sparkle, washed our hoodies and the bright colours got mixed up in the wash. They all came out brown!"

"Oh, what a shame," Kirsty said.

"Actually, *all* our clothes turned brown in the wash," Yvette said with a sigh.

"Except our outfits for the concert this afternoon," Rick reminded her. "Don't forget we're collecting them from Suzy after breakfast."

"That's lucky," remarked Emilia. "Groove Gang just wouldn't be the same if you didn't each have your special colours to wear."

Kirsty looked at the members of Groove Gang. "Would you mind if Rachel and I took a photo of you?" she asked politely.

"Not at all," Priya replied with a smile. "But maybe you'd like to wait until later, when we've changed into our concert outfits?"

"Yes, we'll look more like ourselves then!" Lila agreed. "We'll be wearing our special, signature colours."

"OK," Kirsty agreed.

34

Lexy turned to Rachel and Kirsty. "Sorry, girls, but Serena, Emilia and I aren't looking too great this morning, either!" she said, pointing at her jeans. Rachel and Kirsty saw that they were damp and had muddy stains all over them. Serena and Emilia's jeans were stained too, and there was a big splash of mud on Emilia's white cotton T-shirt.

"What happened?" asked Rachel, taking off her raincoat.

35

"Did you notice that group of boys jumping around in the puddles near Star Village?" Serena asked. The girls nodded.

"Well, they splashed us with muddy water," Lexy sighed.

Rachel and Kirsty exchanged an anxious look. They knew exactly why the pop stars were having such bad luck with their outfits. It was because Miley's magical musical clef was missing! Rachel could feel Miley moving restlessly around inside her shirt pocket, and she guessed that the little fairy was dismayed by what she was hearing.

"Well, Rachel and I had no dry clothes this morning because the rain leaked into our tent," Kirsty explained, hanging her raincoat on the back of her chair. "That's why we're both wearing things that clash!"

Serena smiled. "Let's forget all about our clothes and enjoy a nice brunch together," she suggested as two waitresses came towards them. The waitresses were carrying trays loaded with plates of pancakes, glasses of orange juice and pots of maple syrup, honey and jam which they proceeded to place on the table.

"This looks great!" Blake said eagerly.
He reached for a pancake and then
for a pot of maple syrup, but he ended
up tipping sticky
syrup over his
sleeve. Serena
handed him
a paper
napkin to
clean up, but
accidentally
knocked over

Priya's glass of orange juice. The juice
ran across the tablecloth and dripped
onto Lexy's lap.

Kirsty bit her lip and stole a look at
Rachel as Yvette dropped a blob of
strawberry jam on her knee. The girls
knew that things would only get worse

for the pop stars unless they found Miley's magical clef. But where could it be, Kirsty wondered.

"I think we ought to do some extra rehearsal for the concert this afternoon, guys," Rick remarked when breakfast was nearly over. "Are you all up for it?"

Blake, Priya and Lila nodded.

"Aren't we supposed to be collecting our stage outfits from Suzy now?" asked Yvette.

"We could fetch them for you," Kirsty offered.

"Oh, would you?" Yvette said. "Thanks, girls, it would give us more time to rehearse. Could you collect them from Suzy's trailer and bring them over to the dressing-rooms behind the main stage, please?"

"No problem," said Rachel.

Kirsty, Rachel, The Angels and Groove Gang walked back to the festival site together. It was still raining but not quite so heavily.

"Suzy Sparkle's trailer is that pink, sparkly one over there," Rick told the girls. "Thanks again."

"Thanks for brunch!" Rachel and Kirsty called as Groove Gang went off to their rehearsal tent and The Angels headed for their trailer. When they were alone, Miley popped her head out of Rachel's pocket.

"Isn't it a shame about their lovely clothes?" Miley sighed. "We've got to make sure that *nothing* spoils Groove Gang's outfits for the concert this afternoon — and that means finding my clef. I can feel that it's here somewhere, close by."

"There must be goblins around here, too," Rachel said as they went over to the bright pink trailer.

"We haven't seen any so far today," Kirsty said.

Miley ducked out of sight again as Kirsty knocked on the glossy pink door.

A young woman with long blonde hair, wearing a black lace dress, opened it. "Groove Gang have asked us to collect their outfits for this afternoon and take them to the dressing-rooms," Kirsty explained.

"They've decided to go and rehearse before the concert," Rachel added.

"Oh, do come in." Suzy Sparkle smiled at them. "You're Rachel and Kirsty, aren't you? I've heard all about you from The Angels." She ushered the girls into the caravan which had clothes piled up everywhere. "Look, these are the Gang's outfits," Suzy went on, pointing at a rail with three short black skirts and two pairs of black trousers hanging on it.

Next to them were five colourful shirts. "What do you think, girls?"

"They're fantastic!" Rachel exclaimed. The shirt material was shot through with metallic threads that glittered in the light.

"*And* they're all the right colours," Kirsty said happily, touching the sleeve of Priya's pink shirt. Relieved, she glanced at Rachel. There was nothing wrong with *these* outfits.

Carefully Suzy began removing the clothes from the rail and Rachel and Kirsty hung them neatly over their arms.

"Thanks, girls," Suzy said. "At least it's stopped raining! See you at the concert."

Rachel and Kirsty left the trailer with the outfits. As they headed towards the dressing-rooms, Miley peeped out again.

"The shirts are fabulous, girls!" she declared with a big smile. "We *must* keep them safe –"

"HEY!"

A loud voice nearby made Rachel and Kirsty jump. Then they saw one of the boys they'd noticed earlier come running towards them, with his rain-hat jammed down and his bright green mac flapping around him.

"Look at those shirts!" the boy yelled. "They're amazing!"

Suddenly the other boys appeared and rushed towards Rachel and Kirsty.

The girls were too surprised to move,
and the boys gathered around them,
jumping in the muddy puddles and
trying to grab the outfits. To Rachel
and Kirsty's horror,
they were knocked
backwards into
an enormous,
dirty puddle,
splashing
not only
themselves,
but also the
clothes they
were carrying.

"Oh no!" Rachel gasped, staring down
at the wet and stained shirts, skirts and
trousers. "What are Groove Gang going
to wear for their concert *now*?"

Gorgeous Goblin!

"Look what you've done!" Kirsty cried, staring crossly at the boys. "You've ruined all the outfits!"

Laughing, the boys spun around and ran off, jumping in more puddles as they went. However, one of them was left behind because his welly was stuck in a big patch of boggy mud. Muttering to himself, he tried to yank his boot free.

Instead, his enormous
foot jerked up
and left its welly
behind. Kirsty
and Rachel could
hardly believe their
eyes when they saw
that his skin was *green*.
"He's a goblin!" Kirsty
whispered to Rachel.

"*All* those boys must be goblins, and
we didn't even realise!" Rachel replied.
"But which one of them has Miley's
magical musical clef?"

"Rachel, look at his welly," Kirsty
murmured as the goblin finally rescued
his boot and jammed it back onto his
foot. "It's clean and shiny, even though
it's been stuck in the mud."

"His mac's really clean, too, although he's been splashing around in puddles like the others," Rachel pointed out. "Could he have the clef, and it's stopping his clothes getting messy?"

"I think he has, girls," Miley exclaimed. "Don't let him get away!"

The goblin was racing off now, looking for the others. He ran towards Star Village and then disappeared into the dressing-up tent. Rachel and Kirsty were close behind him, but when they reached the entrance to the tent, they stopped.

"There are lots of people inside," Rachel whispered to Miley. "We don't want anyone to guess what we're up to."

"I'll turn you into fairies then," Miley whispered back, "But hurry, girls!"

Rachel and Kirsty dived behind a nearby trailer. There Miley whizzed out of Rachel's pocket, and then a shower of glittery magic shrank the girls down to Miley's size, with the same fairy wings on their backs. Silently the three friends fluttered into the dressing-up tent, keeping high above the heads of the crowd.

They could see the goblin ahead of
them, weaving his way between the rails
packed with clothes towards the
fitting-rooms at the other end of the tent.

"Where's he gone?" Miley asked a few
minutes later. "Oh dear, I think we've
lost him, girls."

Rachel and Kirsty anxiously looked
all around.

"I can see him!" Kirsty
announced suddenly.
"Well, I can see
his feet, at least!
Look, there are
his big green
wellies poking
out from under
that fitting-room
door."

"The goblin must have jumped the queue," Rachel remarked as they flew over the heads of a long line of people clutching the outfits they'd chosen and waiting to use the fitting-rooms. "I wonder what outfit he's taken in there?"

A moment later the fitting-room door was flung open. Miley, Rachel and Kirsty hovered above, watching as the goblin strutted out. He was wearing a glittering green jacket and trousers, white gloves, dark shades and a black, wide-brimmed hat pulled down over his face.

He looked extremely stylish, and everyone in the queue stared at him admiringly.

"That guy looks fantastic!" Rachel heard a teenage boy say to his friend. The boy was wearing a blue tracksuit that was too big for him and a baseball cap that was too small. "He's got to be the best-dressed person here."

His friend, who was wearing a bright yellow tracksuit, purple trainers and a bowler hat, nodded.

"Everyone else's outfits are rubbish compared to his, aren't they?" he replied. "Including ours!"

As Rachel stared at the goblin, her heart began to hammer with excitement. She could see the magical musical clef hanging on a chain around his neck!

Silently Rachel beckoned to Miley and Kirsty, and together the three of them flew down to land on a shelf stacked with colourful silk and chiffon scarves.

54

Meanwhile the goblin was parading up and down, pretending that he was modelling on a catwalk. Everyone watching applauded enthusiastically.

"The goblin's wearing the clef!" Rachel murmured to Miley and Kirsty. "But how are we going to get it back with all these people around?"

Photo Opportunity

Rachel, Miley and Kirsty thought about it for a moment.

"I *think* I have an idea," Kirsty said slowly. "Listen, here's what I think we should do…"And quickly she explained her plan.

After taking several bows, the goblin had now whisked off into the fitting-room again, leaving the crowd waiting impatiently to see his next outfit.

Quietly Rachel and Kirsty flew down and landed on the floor behind a rail packed with clothes. Still perched on the shelf above them, Miley waved her wand and a cloud of magical sparkles floated down around the girls. Within seconds they were back to their normal size.

Suddenly the crowd cheered. Rachel and Kirsty popped out from behind the clothes rail and saw that the goblin had come out of the fitting-room and was swaggering around again. This time he was wearing a glittery blue shirt, black trousers, gold bracelets and the same black hat.

"Ready, Rachel?" Kirsty whispered, taking her camera out of her pocket. Rachel nodded and did the same. Then the two girls stepped out in front of the goblin.

"Hi, we're taking pictures for a new magazine called *Star Style*," Kirsty said quickly. "We'd love to take some shots of you."

"Your outfit's great," Rachel added. "You're so stylish. You *have* to be in our magazine!"

The goblin preened himself. "Yes, I *am* rather stylish, aren't I?" he said smugly. He put his hands on his hips and posed, and Kirsty and Rachel began snapping away. The crowd watched with interest.

"That's brilliant," Kirsty said, "You should be a model!"

The goblin looked very pleased with himself.

"Can we try something a little bit different?" Rachel asked.

She took a red sequinned scarf from the shelf where Miley was still hiding. "I think this would look lovely in the photos. Could you swap it for that necklace you're wearing now?"

The goblin frowned and touched the magical musical clef hanging around his neck. Rachel and Kirsty waited patiently, trying not to give the game away.

Then, to the girls' dismay, the goblin simply tied the scarf around his neck, over the necklace. Kirsty and Rachel exchanged worried glances. The plan hadn't worked! Now they'd have to come up with something else.

"OK, let's have lots of different poses," Kirsty called, trying to keep the goblin interested to give them time to think. "Look this way and smile. Now, wave at the camera. Stand on one leg…"

The goblin was happy to do everything Kirsty asked. He loved being the centre of attention. But Kirsty was beginning to panic because she simply couldn't think of another way to get the clef back.

"I've got an idea!" Rachel whispered. She murmured a few words to Kirsty, who nodded, and then glanced up at the shelf. Miley was peeping out from behind a pile of scarves and Rachel winked at her.

"I want a really
good shot for the
front page of
the magazine,"
Kirsty called
to the goblin.
"Can you do a
handstand?"

"Of course I
can!" the goblin
retorted. He flung
himself forward
onto his hands and
balanced upside down,
waving his legs in the air. Kirsty watched
with wide eyes as the sequinned scarf
slipped over his head and onto the floor.
Then the necklace did exactly the same!

Groove Gang Rock!

Rachel glanced up at Miley who instantly launched herself off the shelf, hidden underneath a thin, lavender-coloured scarf. The scarf floated down and landed on top of the necklace. Kirsty breathed a sigh of relief and dashed forward to scoop up the scarf, along with Miley and the magical clef, now back to its Fairyland size. Then she popped the fairy safely into her raincoat pocket.

The goblin gave a shriek and overbalanced, falling sideways. Rachel and Kirsty saw the glitter fade from his clothes, and the outfit that had previously looked so stylish, now looked ridiculous and a very bad fit.

"I don't know why we all thought that guy was so stylish," Rachel heard the teenage boy murmur to his friend. "That's the worst outfit I've ever seen!"

The rest of the crowd had lost interest in the goblin, too, as they began to discover all the gorgeous outfits now hanging on the rails. Rachel and Kirsty went over to help him to his feet.

"No one likes my outfits any more," the goblin grumbled.

"Oh, well, you know how fashions come and go," Kirsty said to him.

"But *your* style will last forever!" Rachel told him. "Remember, you just have to be true to yourself, and don't follow the crowd."

The goblin nodded and hurried away.

"That's a quote from Groove Gang's song, *A Style of Your Own!*" Kirsty laughed.

"Talking of Groove Gang…" Rachel whisked a sparkly pink hoodie and a pair of denim shorts off a nearby rail. "Wouldn't this be perfect for Priya to replace the outfit that got all muddy?"

"Great idea!" Kirsty said. "And I can see something that would suit Blake, too." And she showed Rachel a pair of baggy jeans and a shimmering blue shirt.

"Keep looking, girls," Miley murmured from Kirsty's pocket. "The magic of my clef means that there are lots of wonderful pop star clothes to find!"

The girls hunted around the clothes rails, and soon they'd found stage outfits for all the Groove Gang members in their special colours. They even found a couple of very glamorous dresses for themselves, one silver and one gold. Then they hurried out of the tent, their arms full of gorgeous clothes. Now the rain had stopped and the sun was blazing down brightly.

Just before the concert began, Rachel and Kirsty, wearing their silver and gold dresses, went back to the dressing-rooms. Groove Gang had asked them to help Suzy Sparkle with any last-minute adjustments to their outfits. When the girls arrived, they were thrilled to see that the band were all wearing the clothes they'd chosen for them.

"These replacement outfits are great, girls," said Lila. She did a twirl in her short lilac skirt. "It was very naughty of those boys to splash you with muddy water like that."

"But we actually like this new stuff even better!" Rick exclaimed, showing off the red T-shirt and red and black trousers he was wearing.

Beaming happily, Rachel and Kirsty helped Suzy Sparkle with the girls' hair and make-up. They'd just finished fixing Priya's hair when Blake suddenly exclaimed, "Hey, you girls wanted a photo, didn't you? Give your cameras to Suzy and she'll take a few snaps."

Kirsty and Rachel handed over their cameras and Suzy took some shots of them posing with Groove Gang.

"Thank you!" Rachel and Kirsty said, hardly able to believe their luck.

"Right, we're on!" Yvette said, ushering the others out of the dressing-room. "Enjoy the show, girls."

Rachel and Kirsty hurried out into the field to watch the concert. As Groove Gang ran onstage to wild whoops and loud applause, Miley fluttered out of Kirsty's little gold handbag.

"You look very glamorous, girls!" Miley said with a smile.

"It's nice to dress like a pop star sometimes," Rachel said with a grin, smoothing down her shiny silver dress. "But I think these clothes are for special occasions only!"

"Hello, Rainspell Music Festival!" Blake shouted. "We're really glad to be here, and we just have one thing to say to you – be true to yourself and don't follow the crowd, be stylish and proud!"

The crowd roared its appreciation as Groove Gang launched into their big hit, *A Style of Your Own*. Rachel and Kirsty sang along, dancing around while Miley hovered near them.

"My magic is just enough to make sure Groove Gang's concert is a success,"

Miley remarked happily. "Thank you for helping me find my clef today, girls."

"We still have three clefs to find," Rachel said. "And we're not going to give up until we've got them back, are we, Kirsty?"

Kirsty shook her head as she clapped along to the music. "We *can't* let Jack Frost spoil the rest of the Rainspell Music Festival!" she said firmly. "We'll be on the look-out for another clef tomorrow!"

Now Kirsty and Rachel
must help...

Frankie the Make-up Fairy

Read on for a sneak peek...

The sun was shining on best friends
Rachel Walker and Kirsty Tate. It was
the summer holidays, and they had come
to the Rainspell Island Music Festival
as special guests of their favourite pop
group, The Angels.

The girls were standing among the
cluster of activity tents known as Star
Village. There were tents of every shape
and colour, with fortune-tellers, singing
teachers, musicians and stylists offering
their services for free. It was hard to
know which one to choose!

"Let's try that one," said Rachel.

She pointed to a tent that sparkled in the morning sun. The sign hanging outside said "Glitter & Go", and people were lining up to have their faces painted.

As the girls joined the queue, a group of teenagers walked past, chatting about the famous people they had spotted.

"I heard that Dakota May's here," said one of the boys.

Kirsty and Rachel gasped. Dakota May was one of their favourite pop stars.

"I hope she's going to put on a concert while she's here!" said Kirsty.

They started singing Dakota May's latest song, *The Faces of Me*, and they only stopped when it was their turn to have their faces painted. Giggling, the girls hurried into the tent and perched on high stools.

"Hi, I'm Chloe," said a bubbly dark-haired girl to Rachel. "What would you like today?"

Rachel knew exactly what she wanted!

"Could I have a rainbow across my cheek?" she asked.

"Sure thing," said Chloe, picking up her pot of make-up brushes.

"How about you?" asked the red-headed make-up artist in front of Kirsty. "I'm Dora, by the way."

"I can't decide!" said Kirsty with a smile...

Read Frankie the Make-up Fairy to find out what adventures are in store for Kirsty and Rachel!

Meet the fairies, play games
and get sneak peeks at
the latest books!

www.rainbowmagicbooks.co.uk

There's fairy fun for everyone on
our wonderful website.
You'll find great activities, competitions, stories and
fairy profiles, and also a special newsletter.

Get 30% off all Rainbow Magic books at
www.rainbowmagicbooks.co.uk

Look out for the next sparkly
Rainbow Magic Special!

Robyn the Christmas Party Fairy

Rachel and Kirsty are helping to organise a big Christmas party.
But Jack Frost has stolen Robyn the Christmas Party Fairy's
magical objects! The girls must help Robyn,
before the spirit of Christmas is lost forever...

Out now!

Alexandra the Royal Baby Fairy

Out in May 2013

Also available as an ebook

The whole of Fairyland is very excited - there's going to be a new royal baby! But when the special baby goes missing, Rachel and Kirsty are there to help their friend, Alexandra the Royal Baby Fairy.

www.rainbowmagicbooks.co.uk

Meet the
Princess Fairies

Honor
the Happy Days
Fairy

Demi
the Dressing-Up
Fairy

Anya
the Cuddly Creatures
Fairy

Elisa
the Adventure
Fairy

Lizzie
the Sweet Treats
Fairy

Maddie
the Playtime
Fairy

Eva
the Enchanted Ball
Fairy

Jack Frost has stolen the Princess Fairies'
tiaras. Kirsty and Rachel must get them back
before all the magic in the world fades away!

www.rainbowmagicbooks.co.uk